NOV 9 1998

P9-CFG-435

CHICKEN SOUP for LITTLE SOULS

The Never-Forgotten Doll

Story Adapted from
"A Doll for Great-Grandmother"
by Jacqueline Hickey

Story Adaptation by
Lisa McCourt

Illustrated by
Mary O'Keefe Young

HCI

Health Communications, Inc.
Deerfield Beach, Florida

Library of Congress Cataloging-in-Publication Data

McCourt, Lisa.
    Chicken soup for little souls : the never-forgotten doll / story adaptation by Lisa McCourt ;
illustrations by Mary O'Keefe Young.
        p.   cm.
    "Based on the . . . best-selling series Chicken soup for the soul by Jack Canfield and Mark
Victor Hansen."
    Summary: Ellie's love for Miss Maggie, her babysitter, helps her find a way to give Miss Maggie
the best birthday present ever.
    ISBN 1-55874-507-6 (hardcover)
    [1. Babysitters—Fiction. 2. Friendship—Fiction. 3. Dolls—Fiction. 4. Gifts—Fiction. 5.
Birthdays—Fiction.] I. Young, Mary O'Keefe, ill. II. Canfield, Jack, date. Chicken soup for the
soul. III. Title.
    PZ7.M13745Chg   1997
    [E]—dc21   97-19961
                                                                                                                        CIP
                                                                                                                        AC

©1997 Health Communications, Inc.
ISBN 1-55874-507-6

All rights reserved. No part of this publication may be reproduced, stored in a retrieval system or
transmitted in any form or by any means, electronic, mechanical, photocopying, recording or
otherwise, without the written consent of the publisher.

Story adapted from "A Doll for Great-Grandmother" by Jacqueline Hickey, *Chicken Soup for the
Woman's Soul*, edited by Jack Canfield, Mark Victor Hansen, Jennifer Read Hawthorne and Marci
Shimoff.

Story Adaptation ©1997 Lisa McCourt
Illustrations ©1997 Mary O'Keefe Young

Cover Design by Cheryl Nathan

Produced by Boingo Books, Inc.

Publisher: Health Communications, Inc.
             3201 S.W. 15th Street
             Deerfield Beach, FL 33442-8190

Printed in Mexico

For Bettye McCourt and Polly and Robert Hogan,
with all the love in a once-little girl's heart.
—L.M.

For Ora and Dana,
for allowing me to share their beauty with the world.
—M.O'K.Y.

Engleton 14 95

7/21/98

M1375c

"Ellie! What a surprise!" said Miss Maggie when she opened the door. She always said that, even though I came every day after school.

"I've just made cookies," she said. "Will you help me eat a few?"

Miss Maggie was the best sitter I'd ever had, and I'd had a lot. Mom called her my adopted grandmother, but I didn't know you could adopt a person so old.

"Tell me a story from when you were little," I begged Miss
Maggie for the gazillionth time.

"Wonderful idea! What should the story be about
today?" she asked between sips of hot cocoa.

I tried to think up a new story-starter. Miss Maggie's

stories were the best. "I know!" I said. "Tell me about your favorite toy."

Miss Maggie thought for a moment, then frowned. "I should warn you. This one isn't a happy story."

"It's okay. Tell me," I said.

"On my eighth birthday, I opened a present that I will never forget. She was the most beautiful doll I had ever seen. Her big blue eyes opened and closed on a real china face. She wore a fancy white dress with lace trim, and her long brown hair was tied back with a pink satin ribbon. Owning a doll like that was a dream come true for a poor farm girl like me. I knew my parents couldn't afford fine things. How much they must have loved me to have spent their hard-earned money on such a luxury!"

Miss Maggie got a misty look in her eyes. "I was extra-careful with her all morning. Dolls back then were very fragile—their faces were made of the most delicate china. I still remember how magical it felt just to hold her. She was the most wonderful thing I had ever owned. My mother lit the candles on my birthday cake and called me to the kitchen.

"I laid her down gently on the hallway table. But as I went to join my family for my birthday song, we heard the crash. I knew without looking that it was my precious doll! Her lacy dress had hung from the table just enough for my baby sister to reach up and pull on it. When I ran to the hall, there was my doll, her face smashed to pieces. My mother tried to glue her up, but it couldn't be done. She was gone forever."

I had never seen a look like that on Miss Maggie's face. I wrapped my arms around her neck and hugged her tight. The rest of the day we practiced my spelling words and played games, but I couldn't stop thinking about how unhappy Miss Maggie had looked remembering her broken doll.

Later that night, Mom said, "Saturday is Miss Maggie's birthday. Why don't you and I bake her a cake and bring it over there?"

"Oh, Mom, that's perfect!" I said. "Miss Maggie was sad today, and that's just the thing to cheer her up!"

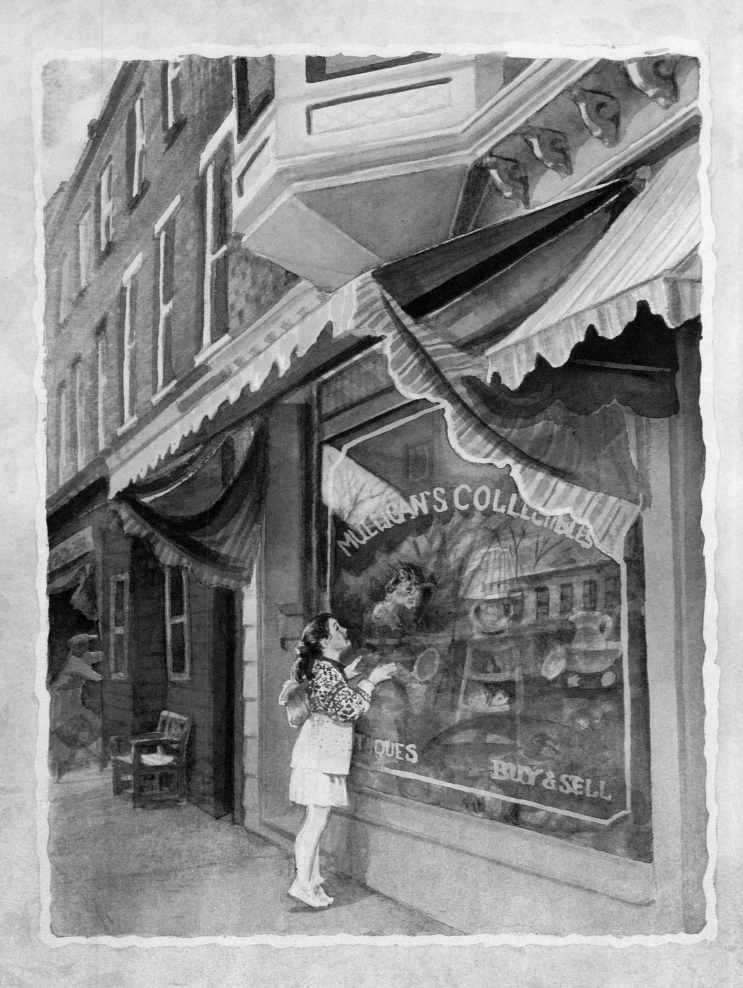

The next day after school, I found an even better thing. I was walking to Miss Maggie's, just like always, when I saw a doll in the window of Mulligan's Collectibles. She looked really old and she had on a white lacy dress. Her hair was blond, not brown, and there was no pink satin ribbon, but I thought Miss Maggie might like her anyway.

I went in and asked Mr. Mulligan, "The doll in the window—do her eyes open and close?"

Mr. Mulligan said, "Yes, they do. But that's not a doll for little girls like you. That's an antique. Grown-ups collect them."

"Oh, it's not for me. I want to buy that doll for my friend, Miss Maggie," I explained.

"That's an awfully expensive present. Maybe Miss Maggie would like one of these embroidered hankies instead." Mr. Mulligan held up a dumb white handkerchief with flowers on it.

"How much for the doll?" I asked him in my most grown-up voice.

"Well, she's not in the best shape. I suppose I could let you have her for thirty-five dollars."

My eyes bugged out about a mile. Where would I ever get thirty-five dollars?

RETA E. KING LIBRARY
CHADRON STATE COLLEGE
CHADRON, NE 69337

That night, I tried Mom. "May I have thirty-five dollars to buy Miss Maggie a birthday present?" I asked, real casual.

Mom laughed. "It's sweet that you want to buy a gift for your friend. But I'm sure the birthday cake we're making will be enough."

I begged and pleaded, but the best I could get out of Mom was: "If you really want to give Miss Maggie a gift that badly, we'll go shopping on Saturday morning. But we can't afford to spend thirty-five dollars. I'm sorry, darling, but we just can't."

I knew no other gift would do, so I emptied my elephant bank and counted my money. I had exactly eight dollars and forty-nine cents.

It was already Thursday. There was no time to save up
any more. I put the eight dollars and forty-nine cents in a
sock and folded it up. I had a plan, but I wasn't sure it
would work.

On Friday after school, I went to see Mr. Mulligan.

"I really need that doll, Mr. Mulligan," I said. "I have eight dollars and forty-nine cents to pay you right now, and I will help out in your store every weekend until I have paid the rest of the money, which will probably be forever."

Mr. Mulligan scratched his head. "After you asked about that doll yesterday, I went to take another look at her. And it's the darndest thing—she's more damaged than I thought. One of my workers must have laid her head on some wet wood stain. The back of her hair is just ruined. I don't know who's going to pay much for her now. I reckon if you need her that badly, I can consider eight dollars and forty-nine cents a fair price."

"You've got a deal!" I shouted.

When Mr. Mulligan took down the doll, and showed me her "ruined" hair, I got the best idea ever!

The time passed slowly at Miss Maggie's that afternoon. When she asked me what was in the bag, I told her it was a secret and she mustn't look inside.

"Aren't you mysterious today?" she teased.

When I got home, I raced to my room and unwrapped the doll. I took out my brown magic marker. I laid the doll down and spread out her hair on a piece of construction paper.

Then, very, very carefully, I colored all of her blond hair brown. The stained part disappeared and she was even more like the doll Miss Maggie remembered!

There was only one thing missing and I knew where to get it. I took my favorite and only party dress out of my closet and laid it on my bed. There, right at the neck, was a pink satin ribbon.

I cut it off with my safety scissors, being careful to cut just the threads that held it on, and not the dress. I tied it in the doll's new brown hair. She was perfect! But what would Mom say when she found out about my dress?

On Saturday, we went to see Miss Maggie.

"Ellie, what a surprise!" she said. For once, I think she meant it.

Mom and I marched in, singing, "Happy birthday to you..." I could hardly wait till the song was over to give Miss Maggie her present!

Miss Maggie carefully pulled back the tissue paper.
When she finally saw the doll, her eyes filled up with tears.
"Ellie," she whispered, "where on Earth..."
"Is she close?" I asked. "Is she like the doll that got
broken?"

"She is exactly like my doll," Miss Maggie said, without once taking her eyes off the present. "But where did you ever find her and how did you ever afford her?"

Mom was looking at me like she wanted to know the same thing, so I told them both the whole story. When I got to the part about my dress, I asked Mom, "Are you mad?"

Mom squeezed my hand and her voice cracked when she told me, "No, sugar, I'm not mad."

A tear ran down Miss Maggie's face and she said, "Now I know how it is possible that this doll looks just like the one I held in my arms exactly eighty years ago today. Both dolls were gotten from pure love. And love, wherever it comes from, always looks the same."

The cake was delicious, and Miss Maggie said it was her favorite birthday yet.